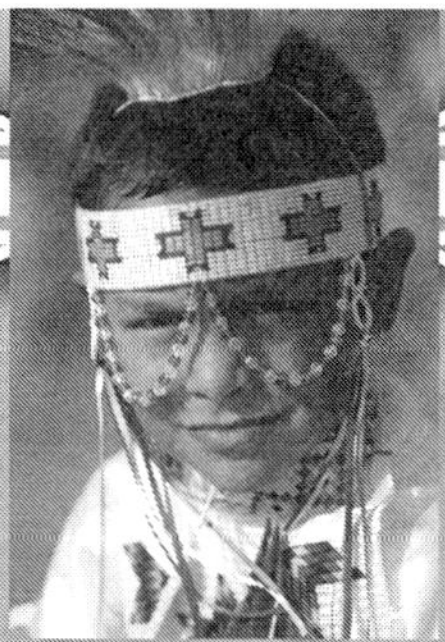

Arkansas Native Americans

A Kid's Look at Our State's Chiefs, Tribes, Reservations, Powwows, Lore, and More From The Past and the Present

By Carole Marsh

Native American Heritage™

Graphic Design: Lynette Rowe • Cover Design: Victoria DeJoy

NATIVE AMERICAN HERITAGE™

CAROLE MARSH BOOKS

Published by
GALLOPADE™ INTERNATIONAL
800-536-2GET
www.gallopade.com

Gallopade is proud to be a member of these educational organizations and associations:

The National School Supply and Equipment Association (NSSEA)
American Booksellers Association (ABA)
Virginia Educational Media Association (VEMA)
Association of Partners for Public Lands (APPL)
Museum Store Association (MSA)
National Association for Gifted Children (NAGC)
Publishers Marketing Association (PMA)
International Reading Association (IRA)
Association of African American Museums (AAAM)

Native American Heritage™ Series

Native American
Big Activity Book

Native American
Biographies

Native American
Coloring Book

Native American
Heritage Book

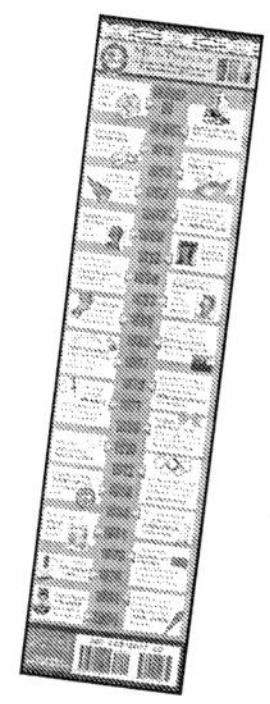

Native American
Timeline

Arkansas State Stuff™

- My First Pocket Guide: Arkansas
- My First Book About Arkansas
- Arkansas Coloring Book
- The Big Arkansas Reproducible Activity Book
- Jeopardy: Answers & Questions About Our State
- Arkansas "Jography!": A Fun Run Through Our State
- Arkansas Gamebooks
- Arkansas Bingo Games
- Arkansas Illustrated Timelines
- Arkansas Project Books
- Arkansas Bulletin Board Set
- Arkansas PosterMap
- Arkansas Stickers
- Let's Discover Arkansas! CD-ROM

Word from the Author

Hello!

I hope you are as interested in North America's wonderful Indian heritage as I am!

Like most kids, I grew up thinking of Indians as the other half of Cowboys. Today, of course, we are getting a much clearer and more accurate picture of what the first peoples on our land were all about. These "facts" are much more fascinating than anything Hollywood can make up. And you probably won't find much of this information in your history textbook!

I am 1/16 Cherokee. This is something I am very proud of and happy about. My grandmother was 1/4 Cherokee. She had tan skin, long gray hair and a very Indian look – especially if I did something bad! Her maiden name was Carrie Corn. Of course, when she got married, she took her husband's name, so it was many years before I learned to appreciate the significance of my native heritage.

Today, I'm trying to make up for lost time by exploring my roots as deeply as I can. One of the most interesting things I've learned is how fascinating all of the Indian tribes are – in the past, the present and future!

As you read about "your" Indians, remember that all native peoples were part of an ever-changing network of time, ideas, power and luck — good and bad. This is certainly a history that is not "dead," but continues to change – often right outside our own back doors! – all the time.

Carole Marsh
She-Who-Writes

PS: Many references show different spellings for the same word. I have tried to select the most common spelling for the time period described. I would not want to be in an Indian spelling bee!

A is for . . .

Amaye

Former Indian town in southwestern Arkansas around 1542.

Aquixo

Indian village once located near the St. Francis River in Arkansas.

Adze

An Indian woodworking tool used to cut, scrape, or gouge; often used to hollow dugout canoes. Blades were made of stone, shell, bone or copper.

Arkansas

The state and river are named for the Quapaw Indians, who were known as the Arkansas by the Illinois Indians. Some say the French first called them Arkansas, with arc meaning bow, placed before the name Kansa.

Aguacay

Large Indian village on the Ouachita River around 1542. Important because salt was manufactured here and traded.

Altar

A platform made of rocks or animal skulls; some had bowls, feathers, rattles, or skins on them. Indians prayed at these altars for things like good crops or expert hunting skills.

Arrow

A long, slender shaft made of reed, cane, or wood; pointed tip was attached to one end and split feathers to the other. Feathers helped the arrows fly straight.

Artifacts

Some of the many prehistoric artifacts that have been unearthed in Arkansas are expertly chipped spear points, found at the Toltec Mounds which date from A.D. 700-950 and from 1100-1300.

Aborigine

A member of the earliest known population of a region.

Arrowhead

The pointed tip of an arrow, made of bone, antler, wood, or iron. Some tips had barbs that would embed themselves in flesh. These barbs made it difficult for an enemy to remove the arrowhead from a wound.

B is for . . .

Burial Mounds

Like some other Indian groups in North America, some Arkansas Indians buried their dead in huge, earthen hills. They were made by piling basketfuls of soil on the gravesites of their dead.

Band

A subdivision of an Indian tribe. In earlier times, a band was sometimes created when part of a tribe split off from the main group. The band also chose new leadership.

Blankets

Used for door covers, partitions, bags, to dry food on, carry babies and many other purposes.

Baskets

Some were woven and others were coiled. Baskets were made from roots, grasses, barks, and other natural materials.

Bullroarer

Sacred instrument symbolizing rain, lightning and thunder. Made of a rectangular piece of wood and a cord. The wood is pine or fir and should come from trees that have been struck by lightning. A person would twirl the wooden part above the head, holding onto the cord.

Buckskin

Softened, smoke-treated rawhide. Used by Arkansas Indians to make clothes, bags and pouches.

Bow

Made from wood, horn or bone. Arkansas Indian children learned how to use bows. The bowstring was made from animal gut, rawhide or twisted vegetable fibers.

Bone

Animal bones were used by Arkansas Indians to make buttons, whistles and other items.

Beads

Made of wood, shells, claws, minerals, seeds — you name it! Later, the Arkansas Indians traded with white men for glass beads, used in some of their decorative arts.

C is for . . .

Chief

Leader of a tribe. Different titles meant different things. Some members were made chief because they owned deeds to land. Chieftainship was often inherited, usually from the mother!

Contact Period

What historians call the era in the 1500s when Native Americans first met Europeans. This meeting changed the lifestyle of the Arkansas Indians more than anyone could ever have anticipated!

Canoe

The Indians invented this useful boat. The "rough" side of the canoe was on the outside, not the inside!

Cave and Bluff Dwellers

Some of the early peoples in Arkansas made their homes in the caves and bluffs of northwest Arkansas, around 8000 B.C. Woven cloth, woven grass baskets and wooden objects have been found in their shelters.

Caddo

Indians who once lived near the mouth of the Red River in Arkansas. Built cone-shaped grass lodges. Had dark skin, pierced their noses and tattooed themselves.

Confederacy

A union of different groups of people. A confederacy in Indian culture was a group of tribes that agreed not to fight with each other. They agreed to live peacefully. Sometimes the tribes shared culture and language.

Clan

A tribal unit. Members are descended from the same ancestor.

Chickasaw

Part of this tribe's ancestral homelands was located in Eastern Arkansas. The fished, hunted and farmed for their food. They were relocated in the 1830s to Indian Territory, and were one of the "Five Civilized Tribes." You can find their descendants in Oklahoma today.

Calumet

Also called "peace pipe" or "war pipe." Refers to the stem of the pipe, which is decorated with feathers or carved to signal the tribe's intentions. Arkansas Indians believed the calumet to have great power.

Chaguate

Village of the southern division of the Caddo tribe on the Ouachita River.

D is for . . .

Dance

There were Indian dances for every occasion: war, peace, hunting, rain, good harvests, etc. Drums, rattles, and flutes of bone or reed provided the music. Dancers often chanted or sang while performing. Steps were not easy to learn and required consistent practice.

Descendants

The first Arkansas Indians were descendants of primitive hunters who crossed the Bering Strait from Asia to what is now Alaska. At that time, glacial ice still covered most of North America. These people were the true discoverers of the "New World!"

Disease

Arkansas Indians had no immunity to the diseases that white explorers, colonists and settlers brought to their lands. These diseases included smallpox, measles, tuberculosis and others, which ravaged the tribes in great epidemics that killed many, and sometimes all, members of a tribe.

Dugout

In 1999, an intact Native American dugout canoe was found on the Saline River. The canoe measured over 23 feet and weighed about a ton. Archaeologists believe it to be a product of the Caddo Indians and dated between 800 to 1,000 years old. It is the oldest complete Native American canoe ever found in Arkansas.

Dyes

Made of lichens, berries, roots, bark, plants, and other natural materials by Indians in Arkansas. Different colors were used depending on what materials were available and what objects were to be dyed.

Dishes

Made from clay, bark, wood, stone, and other materials, depending on what was available and what food they would be used for.

Delaware

Arkansas place named for this Indian tribe.

Dreams

Important in the Indian tradition. It was believed that dreams were the "windows" to the soul. Many thought a person's hidden desires were expressed in dreams.

E is for . . .

Eagle

An animal used in many Indian ceremonies. Eagle feathers attached to war bonnets and shields communicated an Indian's rank in his tribe and what kinds of deeds he had done. Feathers also adorned rattles, pipes, baskets, and prayer sticks.

Early Explorers

Early explorers came to Arkansas such as Hernando de Soto of Spain, and Louis Jolliet and Father Jacques Marquette of France.

Effigy Mound Culture

Built earthen figures of birds, animals or people.

Eastern Indians

By 1000 B.C. Indians in eastern Arkansas had given up their nomadic hunting and gathering lives and settled in villages. They made pottery and cultivated crops for food.

Earrings

Medicine men sometimes pierced male and female ears at special ceremonies. Earrings, which cost parents or relatives a significant amount, symbolized wealth and distinction. The more earrings that an Indian wore, the greater his honor. Some earrings measured 12 inches in length!

Environment

Preserving the environment is important to preserving Native American heritage. For thousands of years, Native American tribes lived completely off the land. Farming, mining, pollution have all had a part in changing native environments.

English

In the 1800s, the U.S. government built boarding schools for Indian children throughout the nation. Children were forced to leave their homes and families to live at these schools. They were required to learn English and not speak their native languages.

Epidemics

Few Indians possessed immunity to the deadly diseases, like smallpox and measles, which European explorers and settlers brought to the New World. As a result, great population loss took place. Sometimes entire tribes became extinct. Epidemics sparked by Hernando De Soto's expedition are estimated to have killed 75% of the native population in the New World.

F is for . . .

Fetish

These small objects were thought to hold the spirit of an animal or a part of nature. A fetish could be an object found in nature, such as bone or wood, or it could be a carved object. The fetish was usually small enough to be carried in a small bag or on a cord. The making and use of a fetish was kept secret by its owner and only shared with the one who inherited it.

Flint

A hard, dull-colored variety of quartz. True flint is found in Arkansas and Texas. The colors are dark gray or dull brown to nearly black. Used by Indians to make flaked tools, knives, arrowheads and spearheads. Hard stones, bones or antlers were used for flaking.

Fishers

Early Arkansas peoples hunted and gathered to keep from starving. Later, they learned to fish. When they finally learned to farm crops, they were more able to settle down into villages, instead of needing to forage all the time.

Farmers

Many Arkansas Indians, ancient and modern, have farming ways! Even pre-contact Indians tilled and irrigated, raising many important crops. Corn, cotton, beans, squash, melons, sunflowers, gourds, pumpkins and tobacco are all native Indian crops!

French and Indian War

Broke out in 1745 over boundary lines between New France and the British colonies. The British defeated the French and their Indian allies. A peace treaty in 1763 ended the war, when Canada and most French possessions east of the Mississippi River were given to the English.

Fire Drill

A device used by Indians to make fires which consisted of a stick and a piece of wood with a tight hole in it. The stick was twirled rapidly in the hole, creating friction that would ignite shredded grass or wood powder placed nearby to start a fire.

Footwear

Arkansas Indians wore different footwear depending on their tribe and environment. Moccasins were made mostly of animal skin. Sandals were made of rawhide or plant material.

Furniture

Arkansas Indian furniture was very simple. Beds were made of skins laid over a frame of wooden slats; the bed posts were driven into the ground. There was often a storage place over the bed to keep personal items. Stools were made of wood, stone and clay.

G is for . . .

Games

Adults played ball and other games of chance or skill. Indian children spun tops, fought pretend battles, did target-shooting, walked on stilts, played hide and seek, or competed to see who could hold their breath the longest!

Ground Grub

The Caddo often looked for acorns and nuts on the ground. These helped make up their food supply.

Gems

Long before the Europeans arrived on the scene, Native Americans discovered pearls in Arkansas. Indians used them for jewelry and personal decoration years before the first explorers came to America!

Gens

Group of related members from different tribes.

Gathering

Native Americans gathered natural materials for food, fuel, baskets, clothing, and housing. American Indians tribes also hunted to meet basic needs. Even though some tribes planted crops, most did some kind of gathering.

Gorgets

Beautiful ornaments hung around the neck or from ears; their significance, if any, is unknown.

Gourds

Hollowed-out shell of a gourd plant's dried fruit which often grew into a specific shape. Indians raised many species of gourds. They were used for spoons, bowls, masks, rattles, and even storage.

Growing Pains

When white settlers first came to Arkansas, there were conflicts when the newcomers tried to clear the Indian hunting grounds for farming. Some white men took Indian wives. Some Indian groups fought among themselves. The Osage Indians of the Ozarks forced the peaceful Quapaws to move south of the Arkansas River. The Caddo Indians, who had been in southwestern Arkansas for hundreds of years, gradually moved south and west into what would become Louisiana and Texas.

H is for . . .

Hatchet

A small, short-handled ax, primarily used as a tool, not as a weapon. When settlers moved in, stone hatchets were replaced with iron ones.

Hair

Indians used hair as a textile. Hair from bison, mountain sheep, elk, moose, deer, dog, rabbit, beaver, or even humans were used to weave cloth, make wigs, or stuff pillows, balls, dolls or drumsticks.

Horn and Hooves

Indians used animal horn to make spoons and dishes. Hooves were made into rattles and bird beaks were used for decoration.

Hampson Museum State Park

Near Wilson, Arkansas. Contains one of the most important collections of Indian artifacts in the South. The items came from the Hampson family's Nodena Plantation. Dr. James K. Hampson excavated more than 1,000 burial sites here. Only a few of the artifacts found at this site are on display, but they are very special. They include jewelry, tools and pottery of the Nodena culture.

Helena

Site of a number of prehistoric Indian burial sites being excavated by archaeologists. A number of such sites have been discovered in eastern Arkansas along the Mississippi River.

Horses

Spaniards brought the horse to America. At first, Indians were afraid of the horse or thought it was sacred. Later, Indians "broke" horses gently, often "hypnotizing" them with a blanket. Horses were used for transportation, trade, barter or payment. Some Indians ate horse meat in hopes of gaining the animal's power.

Hot Springs National Park

Interpretive programs about the life of the Caddo Indians and their predecessors. Explains the use of the thermal springs by the Indians. A museum includes Indian artifacts. They also publish *Indians of Tonico and The Valley of the Vapors*.

Home, Sweet, Home

The Osage lived in oval or rectangular pole-frame houses covered with mats or hides.

Hunters

Early Indian peoples were hunters who used wooden spears with stone points to kill many kinds of large mammals that are extinct today, such as mammoths and mastodons!

I is for . . .

Indian Scout

This term for a guide applied to Indians or white-skinned people who served that role.

Indian Reservation

A tract of land set aside by a government for Indians to live on.

Indian Removal Act of 1830

This federal act gave President Andrew Jackson the power to relocate tribes east of the Mississippi to an "Indian Territory." The forced removal of the southeast Indians later became known as the "Trail of Tears."

Independence

Native American tribes are sovereign nations. That means they are independent. Some even issue their own passports! However, Native Americans are also considered citizens of the United States and enjoy all the rights and privileges of U.S. citizens.

Indian Relations

The Osage Indians had three major groups—the Little Osage, the Great Osage, and the Arkansas Osage. The Little Osages had one village and the Grand Osages had four separate but related villages. They were the Thorny Thickets, the Heart Stays, the Big Hills, and the Upland Forests. The two hereditary chiefs from the Upland Forest village spoke for the whole Osage Tribe in relations with other Native Americans and outsiders. The Arkansas Osage broke off from the Great Osage in the early 1800s, migrating to the Arkansas River.

Indian Ladder

Indians made ladders by trimming branches off a tree. Some were left at consistent intervals to provide steps.

Indian

In 1493, Christopher Columbus called the native people he met in North America "Indians" because he mistakenly believed he had sailed to India! Today, this term includes the aborigines of North and South America.

Indian Tribes in Arkansas

At one time or another, these tribes have lived in the state of Arkansas: Caddo, Chickasaw, Illinois, Osage, Quapaw, Shawnee

J is for . . .

Just So You Know . . .

Today you can find many Arkansas Indians that follow some traditional ways. But there are also many who are entrepreneurs, doctors, lawyers, educators and even politicians! If you visit a reservation or cultural event, make sure you know visitor etiquette. Often dances are religious ceremonies and should be observed as such; religious dances should not be applauded. Photography, videotaping and drawing are all important issues - check with the tribe or individual before any is started.

Jesuits

Roman Catholic priests called Jesuits were among the first to meet and live with the North American Indians. Their writings, sent back to Europe, serve as one of today's best references to early Indian life.

Justice?

For hundreds of years, Native Americans have not received justice from federal and state governments. Native Americans have had nearly all their land taken away. Native Americans still have to fight for their rights in courts across the land.

Judicial Termination

Modern term to describe current efforts by various U.S. government agencies and officials (especially the judicial system) to legally decrease the sovereignty of independent Indian tribes.

Just In Time!

The Indian Arts and Crafts Act of 1990 makes it against the law to pretend that an item has been made by Native Americans if it is really not. It is illegal to offer or display for sale, or sell any art or craft product in a way that falsely suggests it is Indian produced.

Jerked Meat

Thin strips of buffalo, elk, deer or other animal meat which is dried on racks in the sun; also called "jerky."

K is for . . .

Ka-Do-Ha Indian Village

Murfreesboro; prehistoric Caddo Indian grounds and a museum housing artifacts from the excavation of the site.

Kill Site

An archaeological site where remains of many animals have been found along with human artifacts. Many kill sites have been useful to scientists in learning how ancient American Indians lived.

Killed Pottery

Pottery placed in a grave as an offering to the dead person was called killed pottery. A hole was formed in its base during creation. Often broken pottery was placed in a grave because Indians believed the spirit of the dead person would then be released and could travel.

Knife

Made from various materials such as bone, reed, stone, wood, antler, shell, metal, or animal teeth (bear, beaver, etc.), knives were used as weapons but also creative handiwork.

Knowledge

Knowledge is power. Native Americans shared knowledge with the first European settlers. Native Americans showed settlers how to plant crops, which plants were safe to eat, and other knowledge about the land.

Knots

Tied on bowstrings, spearhead and arrowhead lashings, snowshoes, and other items, knots were sometimes used to keep track of the days like a calendar—each knot equaled one day.

L is for . . .

Linguistic Families

There are 56 related groups of American Indian languages. A few of these speech families include Iroquoian, Algonquian, Siouan, Muskogean, Athapascan, and Wakashan.

Leggings

Both men and women wore cloth or skin covering, which were often decorated with quills, beads, or painted designs, for their legs.

Lost Tribes of Israel

This historic theory has been floating around since 721 BC. The 10 lost tribes of Israel are supposedly groups of people gathered together by Sargon, the King of Assyria. Some say he cast out 10 of the 12 tribes of Israel. Many have tried to prove that the American Indians are these missing tribes!

Location

Arkansas Indians before 1700 were mainly on the Arkansas and Red rivers in the southwestern part of the state. By the 1500s, various American Indian groups had settled in many of the nonmountainous parts of the state. Northwestern Arkansas was the hunting territory of the Osage Indians.

Lodge

The term for a type of Indian house that was usually a permanent dwelling. The population of a tribe was often estimated by its number of lodges.

Little Rock

A rocky, moss-covered promontory on the south bank of the Arkansas River was once an important landmark for Indians in the Arkansas River Valley. It marked the point where the vast lowland plains to the east broke into steep and craggy hills. The little rock was partially destroyed during the construction of a railroad bridge. What remains of it can be see in Riverfront Park in downtown Little Rock.

Land Loss

Native Americans lost their land in many ways. Conflicts with other tribes, colonization, European settlement, treaties, and removal took away Indian lands.

Lance

Spear used for hunting and war. The hunting lance had a short shaft and a broad, heavy head. The war lance was light and had a long shaft.

Lariat

These throw ropes made of rawhide, buffalo hair, or horsehair sometimes measured up to 20 feet long!

M is for . . .

Midden Heap

Refuse heaps found along the White, Red and Ouachita rivers that contain empty shells left by early peoples in our state.

Maize

Also called Indian Corn. Known as a "cereal" plant because it probably began as some form of grass. The Indians in our state figured out every possible way to use corn as a food. The only thing the white man added was the creation of "corn flakes!"

Mortar and Pestle

A two-part milling tool, with a bowl-shaped stone, plus a club-shaped stone (or wooden bowl and wooden club), used for pulverizing or grinding plants or animal matter.

Mushalatubbee

Choctaw chief who died of smallpox in Arkansas in 1838.

Medicine

Medicine could be good or bad. Medicines or charms were placed in a bag by young warriors and carried at all times. Some of the roots, leaves and bark that Indians in our state used as medicine are being rediscovered and used by today's doctors!

Moccasins

Indian shoes made of animal skin.

Medicine Man

A person who got the power to heal the sick through a secret means, usually from a dream or visions.

Mound Builders

About 2,000 years ago a wave of migrating people came to our area. They were the first of many groups to be known as the Mound Builders, for the earthenworks they created. Sometimes built high earthen walls around their villages, possibly for defense. They vanished long before the first white explorers reached Arkansas.

N is for . . .

Nomadic

A way of life in which people frequently moved from one location to another in search of food. "Seminomadic" people had permanent villages, but left them in certain seasons to hunt, fish, or gather wild plant foods.

Nodena Culture

These Indians lived in Arkansas between around A.D. 900 and 1540. They grew corn, squash and beans, as well as hunted and farmed. The Nodena site included ceremonial mounds, a central plaza and a playing field. It was surrounded by homes and family burial plots.

Nation

There are many Indian nations located within the United States, such as the Chickamauga Nation. Indian nations are called nations because their governments and laws are independent of and separate from the U.S. government. The federal government must have "government to government" relations with these Indian nations, just as it would with foreign nations, like England or Spain.

Names

Indian names were often changed during one's lifetime. These names could be derived from events that happened during the person's birth, childhood, adolescence, war service, or retirement from active tribal life. Some names came from dreams, some were inherited, and sometimes names were stolen or taken in revenge. Today some Indians maintain old, traditional Indian names, while others take modern names. Since settlers often did not read or write Indian languages, they recorded Indian names phonetically (as they "sounded"). Thus Indian names were often misspelled.

November

In 1990, President George Bush approved a joint resolution designating November 1990 "National American Indian Heritage Month." Similar proclamations have been issued each year since 1994.

National Museum of the American Indian

The Smithsonian's National Museum of the American Indian on the National Mall in Washington, D.C., symbolizes a deeper understanding between America's first citizens and those who have come to make these shores their home.

Necklaces

Some of the Osage Indians made bear claw necklaces decorated with otter fur.

O is for . . .

Ozark Mountain Indians

The Indians that lived in the Ozark Mountain region of Arkansas continued to live as hunters and gatherers for a long time after other Indians in the state had settled into villages.

Old Bones

No one knows for sure when the first people came to North America, but scientists have dated bones and artifacts discovered at Clovis, New Mexico around 11,200 years old. Testing on a skeleton found on the Channel Islands, off the coast of California showed they were about 13,000 years old. And, evidence of human habitation in southern New Mexico suggests that people may have been there as far back as 38,000 years ago.

Origins

Some scientists believe that Native Americans actually came across a land bridge between Asia and North America. They say that during an ice age thousands of years ago, the water level was much lower and people could have walked between the two continents.

Osage

A famous Arkansas Indian tribe. Seminomadic; hunted buffalo and farmed. The tree's wood they prized for making bows is the Osage Orange.

Oil

Indians extracted oil from the many layers of fat that came with fresh bear meat. The fat was boiled down in earthen pots to produce the oil, which was stored in gourds and pots. The oil was used for cooking and even beautifying the body! Indians would mix red pigment with the oil, add the fragrances of cinnamon and sassafras, and rub it all over their bodies.

Orators

Many Indian leaders were excellent public speakers. Powerful and dramatic speakers were vital to leaders who wanted to influence their tribe. Watch for famous Indian quotations in literature and textbooks!

Office of Indian Education Programs

This is a service organization devoted to providing quality education opportunities for American Indian people. Established in the latter part of the nineteenth century to carry out the federal government's education commitment to Indian tribes, it has become the only national education system for American Indian children and adults.

P is for . . .

Powwow

The original form of the word meant "medicine man." Medicine men would often use noise motion and confusion to scare away harmful spirits and cure people. It was also a gathering to talk about political matters. Today, the powwow is an event where Indians gather to sing, perform ceremonial dances, and share cultural pride and traditions.

Parkin, Arkansas

Mound site arranged around a central plaza. Fortifications once surrounded the village and platform-topped mounds. Served as the center of social, government and religious life for people in the area.

Plum Bayou People

Early people of central Arkansas. They lived a stable, settled life. They farmed corn, beans and squash. They also fished and hunted and lived in sturdy houses. Their mound areas were social, religious and political centers.

Paint

Indians used many natural materials to make paint, like clay mixed with oil or grease. Yellow "paint" was made with the gall bladder of a buffalo! Why did they paint their faces or bodies? Indians used paint to look scary or beautiful, to disguise themselves, or to protect their skin from sunburn or insect bites. Indians often applied red paint because it symbolized strength and success. That is why settlers often referred to the Indians as Red Men.

Pemmican

Indian food made of animal meat, which was dried in the sun, pounded together with fat and berries. The mixture was packed into skin bags and used primarily while on the trail.

Papoose

An American Indian infant aged between birth and one year is called a papoose. This word also refers to the way infants were bundled and carried by its mother. A papoose spent most of his or her days snugly wrapped in a kind of cradle made of skins or bark and a wooden frame that hung on the mother's back. This sturdy frame also allowed a mother to lean her papoose against a tree or rock within sight as she worked.

Pottery

Indian pottery was made from built-up spirals of clay that were molded or paddled, or a combination of the two methods. Most pottery served as cooking vessels.

Picture History

Some Indians kept a record of time and important events by painting or drawing pictures or symbols on skin, bark, or stone.

Q is for . . .

Quillwork

Indians used the quills of porcupine or birds to make a type of embroidery. Quills were dyed with juice from berries and other materials. When they were ready to be used, the quills were either mashed with teeth or softened with hot water and flattened with rocks. The quills were then laced into moccasins, shirts, pipe covers, and other items. Beads which Indians received by trading with settlers eventually replaced quillwork.

Quality

Native American arts and crafts are known for their excellent craftsmanship and striking designs. This work is often influenced by things found in nature especially plants and animals.

Quapaw

This tribe's name meant "downstream people." Were called Arkansa or Arkansas by the Illinois and other Algonquian Indians. Lived in walled villages and built large mounds. Considered "troublesome" by white settlers because they balked at giving up their native lands.

Quirt

A short riding whip with a wood, bone, or horn handle.

Quiver

Case used to hold arrows; made of woven plant materials or animal skins.

Quarry Site

A location where Indians went for workable stone such as flint and made stone tools.

Quapaw Line

Once marked the western boundary of treaty lands belonging to the Quapaw Indians. Today the Quapaw Quarter in Little Rock, on the site of this boundary line, is a mixture of historic homes and businesses.

R is for . . .

Rain Dancing

The rain dance ceremony, performed to encourage rainfall, was common among Indian religions because good weather is vital for a successful harvest. Rainmakers were in tune with nature; there are actual reported cases of Indians producing or preventing rain!

Roots

Indians used plant roots for food, medicine, dye, baskets, cloth, rope, salt, flavoring, and just to chew!

Rattles

Indians of Arkansas made rattles from bird beaks, animal hooves, bones, pods, seashells, turtle shells and other animal parts. The rattles are used in ceremonies.

Rock Art

Today, we can still observe Arkansas' prehistoric Native American rock art . This art may have been created by the historic Caddo, Osage, Quapaw, Tunica, and Wichita tribes.

Rawhide

Untanned animal hide. The "green" hide was stretched on the ground or over a frame. Flesh and fat were removed. The skin was dried, washed, then buried with wood ashes which made the hair come off. Used by the Arkansas Indian to make drumheads, lash lodge poles, mend broken objects and in many other ways.

Reservations

The U.S. government set aside, or "reserved," land for the Indians. These reservations originally served as a sort of prison during the beginning stages of Indian removal. At that time, reservations provided the government with some control over Indian activity and residency. This land was usually considerably less desirable land than the Indians' native territories. Today's reservations are lands that are tribally held, yet protected by the government.

Removal

The U.S. government policy of the 1830s-1850s that removed Indians from their native lands to new lands, primarily west of the Mississippi River.

S is for . . .

Sign Language
A way for Indians to communicate with others from a tribe whose language they did not speak.

Shaman
Medicine man and spiritual leader who was supposed to have special healing power from another world.

Secret Societies
Indians had secret groups, usually organized for religious or ceremonial reasons. Each society had a purpose, such as to cure disease.

Shield
A piece of "armor" made of a rawhide-covered frame, which was carried into battle. Shields also could be decorative and religious objects. Many tribes make shields today as an art form!

Sweatlodge
Structure used for ritual purification by sweating from exposure to very hot fires or hot steam from pouring water over hot stones. Also called a sweathouse, for some tribes also doubling as clubhouses.

Stone-boiling
Cooking method by placing preheated stones into cooking vessels.

Shawnee
Indians who migrated from homelands in Kentucky and Tennessee. They split into different groups and migrated often. Introduced cultural traits of the southern tribes to the northern tribes, and vice versa. The Absentee Shawnee lived in Arkansas at one time.

Sacred Bundles
A group of objects treasured by a tribe. They were well-guarded and often taken into battle. The items were publicly shown only on very important occasions.

Saddle
While some Indians did use saddles on their horses, most rode bareback!

Signals
Indian signs made with a pony, blanket, mirror, smoke, fire-arrow or other item to communicate over long distances.

Southern Lowland Indians
Gave up their hunting and gathering life style to farm corn, beans and squash and to hunt game with bows and arrows. Their many styles of pottery indicated that they traded with other Indians throughout the southeastern United States.

Sachem
The supreme Indian ruler of an area where there are many related tribes.

T is for . . .

Tobacco

A sacred plant early Indians used to make offering to their gods, cure diseases, bring good luck, seal agreements and bind treaties.

Treaties

Written agreements between the U. S. government and the Indians, most of which involved the Indians giving up their native lands.

Throwing Stick

A sling or grooved stick used to hurl a lance or spear. It was used by Arkansas Indians before bows and arrows.

Totem

The spirit of some natural object (usually an animal) taken by an Indian, tribe or family to guard over them.

Tahchee

Cherokee Indian chief who lived in Arkansas. He became a scout for the U.S. army and had his portrait painted by famous Indian artist, George Catlin, in 1834.

Tomahawk

A club, axe or hammer used to chop wood, drive stakes in the ground or as a weapon.

Tracking

To follow a trail by finding a sign such as a broken blade of grass, a moved stone or moccasin track. Indians learned to trail as children, so that they could find food, track enemies and disguise their own signs.

Teeth

Arkansas Indians hung teeth on cords to make necklaces.

Tribe

A group of Indians with shared culture, history, original territory, ancestry, social organization, and governmental structure. A tribe may contain several bands of Indians.

Toltec Indian Mounds

In the mid-1800s, Gilbert Knapp discovered huge mounds on his property. Thinking the mounds had been built by the Toltec Indians of Mexico, he named them the Toltec Mounds. Archaeologists later confirmed the mounds were built by the Plum Bayou Culture, probably between A.D. 700 and 950.

Thunderbird

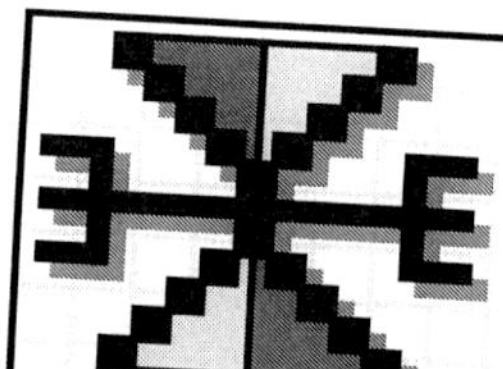

A mythological Indian figure, as well as a part of the constellations for many Indians. Thunderbird mythology is mostly different from tribe to tribe, in general either coexisting with ancestors as an actual bird, or appearing as a spiritual nature god. The Thunderbird was good to the people in either case. Much mythology ties the thunderbird with thunder, lightning and storms.

U is for . . .

Unique

Each and every tribe has its own unique customs, language, and traditions.

U.S. Army

Many Native Americans have fought bravely for the United States Army. Many have also given their lives for a country that was not always accepting of them.

U.S. Bureau of Indian Affairs

Provides public services such as law enforcement, land records, economic development, and education to Indians. Known for mismanagement and ethical problems.

U.S. Indian Schools

The Bureau of Indian Affairs operates hundreds of federal schools around the nation. Enrollment of Native American children measures in the thousands!

U.S. Indian Reorganization Act

Passed by Congress in 1934, the act authorized Indian tribes to establish and conduct their own governments, and to form businesses.

U.S. Colonists

Called Long Knives or Big Knives by early Indians, who also called English explorers "Coat Men."

U.S. Indian Wars

The U.S. War Department has compiled an official list of "Indian Wars" that occurred in the United States. Over 50 wars were fought between the U.S. and the Indians during the period of 1790-1850.

U.S. President

Once called Great White Father by Indians.

V is for . . .

Vessels

Indians carried water in special gourds shaped liked bottles, called water vessels.

Village Councils

These were held in the town (council) house and occurred to discuss and decide important matters. Harmony and agreement was essential to tribal unity. Rather than vote on issues, they were discussed until everyone was satisfied. Anyone who wanted to could speak freely. Everyone did not always agree on the outcome, but everyone avoided conflict by pushing their case.

Vegetable Dyes

Indians could not buy color from the store like we can today. Instead, they created many different colors from the things they found on earth like plants, flowers, shrubs, trees, roots, and berries. They made beautiful and unique reds, oranges, yellows, greens, browns, and violets. These dyes were used for baskets, pottery, weaving, body makeup, and clothing.

Very Hungry

There were Indians who here hunters, gatherers and foragers, that often ate whatever they could find! How hungry would you have to be to eat what they sometimes ate: reptiles, larvae, and insects?

Villages

Many Arkansas Indians lived in villages! Villages were formed around different clans or bands within the tribe, but could also contain different clans living together. Villages were usually permanent settlements, although semi-nomadic tribes have been known to migrate between permanent villages.

Vesperic Indians

Indian tribes located in the United States.

W is for . . .

War Bonnet
Special headdress worn into battle, often adorned with feathers.

War Pony
Horse, often painted with colorful paint and ridden into battle.

Women
Indian women in some Arkansas tribes were poor and hardworking, like the men. But in some tribes, women had many rights, including becoming chief!

War Chief
Historically, Osage Indians had two chiefs and two clans in each village. The Sky People (under the peace chief) lived in the north part of the village, and the Earth People (under the war chief) lived in the south part of the village.

Whistle
Indians from Arkansas made them from the wing bones of birds. The whistles made the sound of the bird the bones came from! Used to communicate, signal, sound an alarm or even flirt with a maiden!

White Man
Indians generally called them Pale Face, a name the white men themselves suggested!

War Club
A weapon made of stone, bone, or wood in the shape of a club.

War Dance
Indian braves danced this before going into battle. The dance was a way of assembling the braves and getting them to commit to the fight ahead.

XYZ are for . . .

Xenophobe

A xenophobe is someone who is afraid of foreign people, their customs and cultures, or foreign things. Many of the first European settlers were afraid of Native American cultures.

You Bet!

Some Native Americans say that Casinos make a lot of money. Others say that too many people have a gambling problem. In the 1980s and 1990s, many tribes discussed whether or not gambling casinos should be allowed. Now that many casinos have been built across the country, the debate has switched to how it should be controlled.

Zounds!

Between 1871 and 1913, at least 98 traditional agreements between tribes and the United States were negotiated and 96 of them were ratified by Congress. Each agreement remains as law (unless changed by a later agreement)!

Yoholomicco

Former chief of the Creek Indians who lived in Arkansas. He was born around 1790. He was a signer of a treaty with whites that ceded lands to the government.

ZZZZZZ...

Shamans and medicine men were not the only people who had access to the spirit world. Indians believed that people could make contact with spirits every night in their dreams! Dreamers could travel back to the time of man's creation or far ahead into their own futures. They also believed that dreams contained warnings or commands from the spirits. Many tribes felt that they had to act out their dreams as soon as they awoke. If an Indian dreamed about bathing, for example, he would run to his neighbors' houses first thing in the morning, and his neighbors would throw kettles full of cold water over him.

Y... Or, "Why?"

1. Why do you think Indian warriors carried charms with them? Some Indian medicines have been scientifically proven to have true healing power and are still used today. Do you think their charms had any real power to help them win battles?
2. Why do you think the American government kept relocating Indians onto reservations and then making the reservations smaller and smaller?
3. Why did Indians use items such as a pipe in ceremonies? What kinds of symbolic objects do we use in ceremonies today?
4. Why and how did Indians use natural materials in creative ways?
5. Many Indian tribes are running successful businesses on their reservations today. There is one industry that many tribes are making a lot of money at. Do you know what this is? Hint: "I'll bet you do!"

Which Famous Native American Am I?

Solve the puzzle!

Word Bank

Black Elk	Crazy Horse	Sitting Bull	Sequoia
Sacajawea	Chief Joseph	Geronimo	Pocahontas

Down

1. This Shoshone woman joined Lewis and Clark as their guide and translator and helped make the expedition a success! Hint: She has 4 "a"s in her name!
4. This man gave the Cherokee their first alphabet so that they could write. Until then, they communicated only by speaking and drawing pictures. Hint: A famous ancient tree also has the same name!
5. He was one of the fiercest of Indian warriors! He fought against white settlers in Arizona and New Mexico to keep his people from being pushed off their lands. Hint: Jump!

Across

2. A legend says that this brave Algonquian woman saved the life of Englishman John Smith. Hint: Disney produced a movie about her.
3. He fought at Little Bighorn when he was only 13! He was also a wise "shaman" who saw visions and could advise people. Hint: Part of his name is an animal with antlers!
6. He was a great Sioux warrior who won the battle against General Custer at Little Bighorn in 1876. Hint: His horse was not crazy!
7. A leader of the Lakota (Sioux) tribe who lived on the Standing Rock Reservation in North Dakota after the battle of Little Bighorn. He tried to make conditions better for his people there, so the U.S. government called him a "troublemaker." Hint: He did not sit all the time!
8. A wise and brave chief of the Nez Percé who tried to bring his people to Canada to escape war. He said, "From where the sun now stands, I will fight no more forever." Hint: His father's name was "Old Joseph."

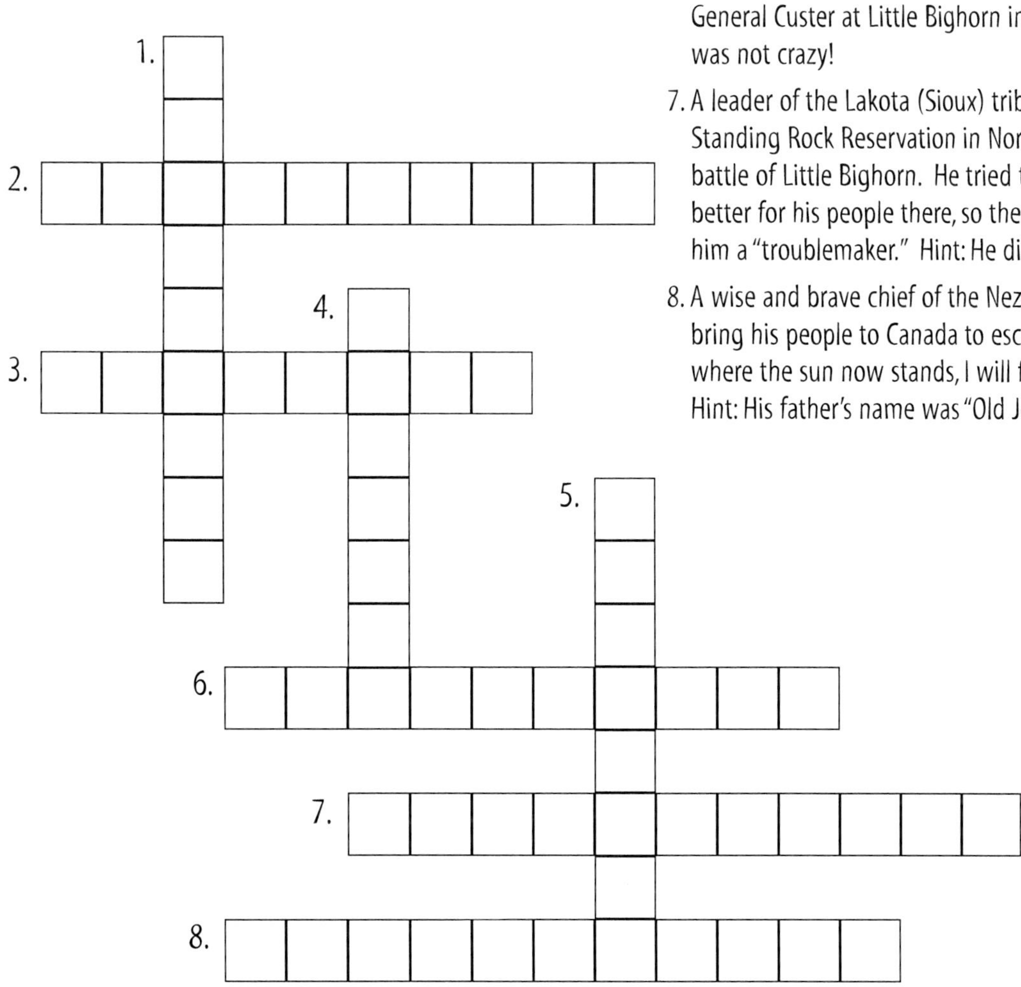

Answer Key: 1. Sacajawea; 2. Pocahontas; 3. Black Elk; 4. Sequoia; 5. Geronimo; 6. Crazy Horse; 7. Sitting Bull; 8. Chief Joseph

Different Ways for Different Indians!

North American Indian tribes are divided into different areas. In each of these areas, tribes shared common ways of living with each other. They might make similar arts or crafts, they might eat the same foods, or they might have had the same beliefs. These activities are all part of their "culture." Each area had its own culture, which was different from the tribes in all the other areas.

Below is a map of all the different groups of Indian tribes in North America. Color each area with a different color. You will see a colorful picture of how Native Americans can all be called "Indians" but still have very different cultures!

Celebration!

Powwows are big festivals where Native Americans gather to sing, dance, and eat together. It is a time to celebrate and show pride in their culture. Powwows can last from one afternoon to several days. The Indians dress in native costumes and dance ancient dances to the beating of drums.

Artists sell their arts and crafts. You might be able to buy some real Native American food cooked on an open fire. Native Americans go to powwows to be with each other, share ideas, and just have fun! Most powwows are also open to people who are not Indian. It's a great place to learn about Native American culture!

If you went to a powwow this weekend, what do you think you would see? What do you think might NOT be there? Circle the objects you think you would see at a powwow. Put an X through those you probably won't see.

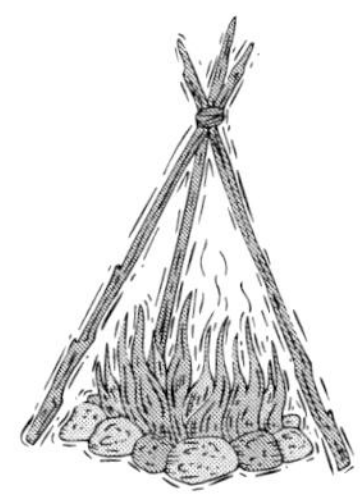

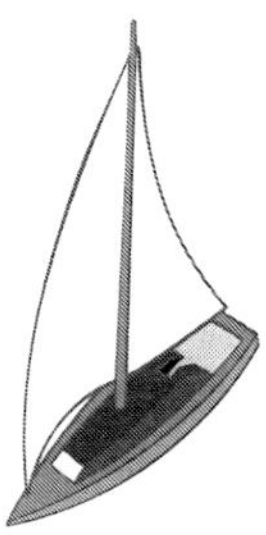

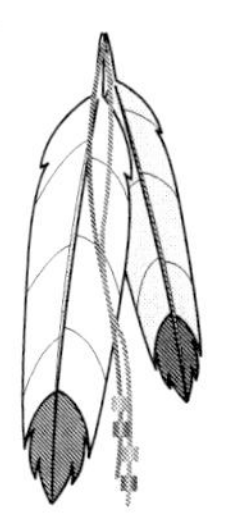

Answer Key: Circled objects are: beads, moccasins, open fire, drums, feathers, baskets, kids, food, drums, horse.

Make an Indian Weaving!

Many Native Americans used weaving to create useful things like sashes (belts), bags, mats, and blankets. They used animal hair to make yarn, and dyed the yarn with natural dyes from fruits and other plants. They also used some plant fibers, like cotton, to make weaving thread.

Weave a small Native American mat of your own. Use different colors of yarn to create a beautiful pattern in your weaving. Place a favorite object on the mat or hang it on your wall!

Prepare the "loom"

Cut a piece of cardboard 5 inches wide and 6 inches long. Along the two 5-inch sides (the "short" sides), have an adult cut slits 1/4 inch deep. These slits should be 1/2 inch apart from each other. So, on each short side you will have 9 slits.

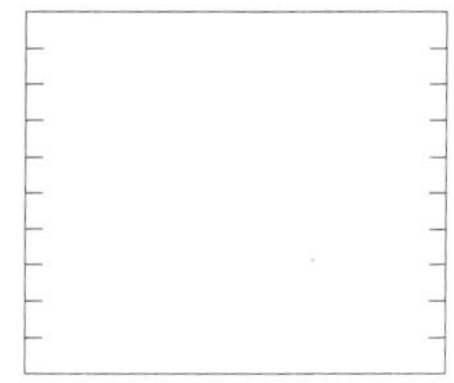

Directions:

1. Take a long piece of yarn and bring it from the back through the first slit (the one next to the edge of the cardboard.) The end of the yarn will hang down behind the cardboard.

2. Bring the yarn right across the front of the cardboard to the slit opposite the one your yarn came through.

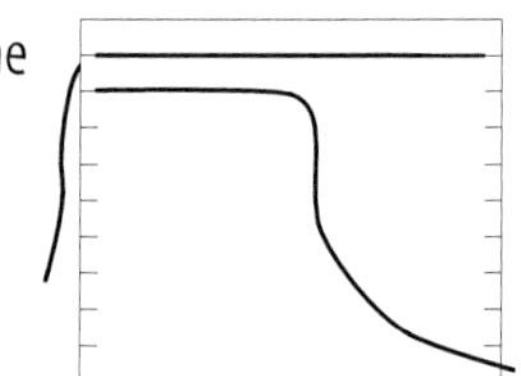

3. Now bring the yarn under the back of the cardboard and then up again through the second slit.

4. Repeat #2 and #3, until you have 9 strands of yarn across the front of your cardboard!

5. Then cut the yarn and tie the two loose ends in the back of the cardboard.

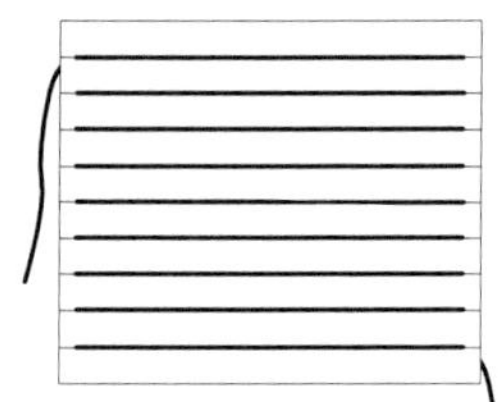

6. Take another piece of yarn and start feeding it through the 9 strands, going over one, under the next over the next, etc. When you get to the end, pull the yarn behind the cardboard and around to the front, and begin again. This time, whatever strand you went over, go under. And whatever strand you went under, go over.

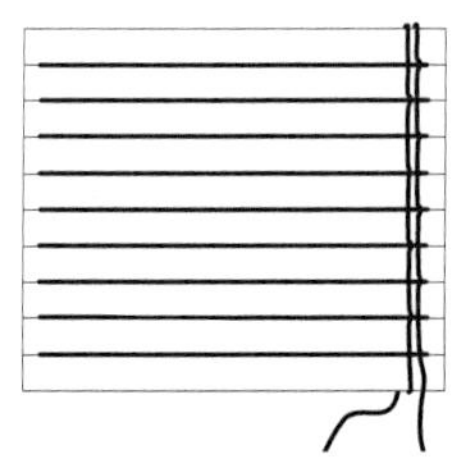

7. Repeat this pattern until the front of your cardboard in covered. Then cut the yarn in the back of the cardboard, and trim it to create a fringe for your mat!

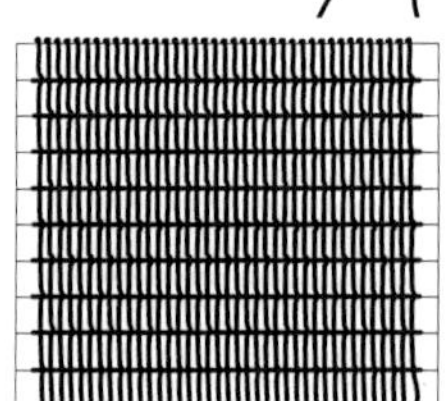

Tips:

- For a wild look, use variegated or different colored yarn!
- For a tighter mat, push the under/over strands up against the previous strands during weaving.
- To keep your mat from unravelling, tie neighboring fringe together up close to the mat.

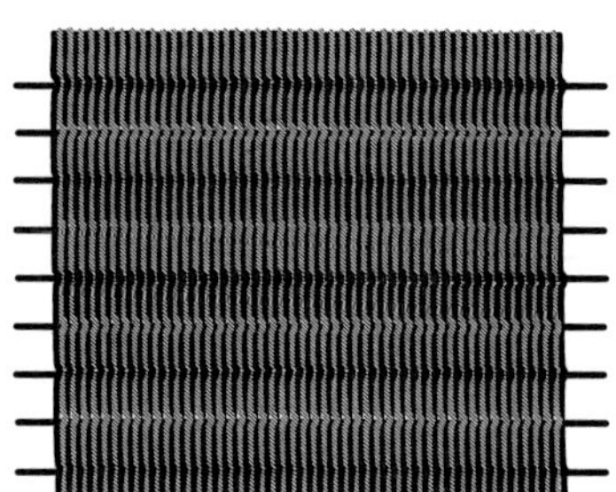

Finders Keepers?

Native Americans have many buried treasures. For hundreds of years, special objects would sometimes be buried with Native Americans, or maybe they would just be lost. Archaeologists used to dig for interesting artifacts in old Native American gravesites. They would keep the Native American bones or the arrowheads, rattles, masks and other objects that they found. But this made the Native Americans feel like they were being robbed.

In 1990, the U.S. government passed a law that said that no one could look for or take these Native American objects anymore. And whoever had any already had to give them back to the people they belonged to. This is called repatriation

Help the archeologist return the artifact to a Native American.

Fast Fact

An artifact is an object that was made by people a long time ago for some useful purpose.

Busy Hands!

Before modern times, Native Americans didn't have stores where they went to buy things. They made everything they needed.

What did Indians make with their own hands? Use the Word Bank and pictures to find out!

Word Bank

blanket	moccasins	arrows	pottery	canoe
mat	food	jewelry	pouch	box

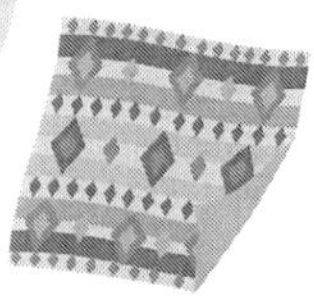 ___ ___ ___

 ___ ___ ___ ___

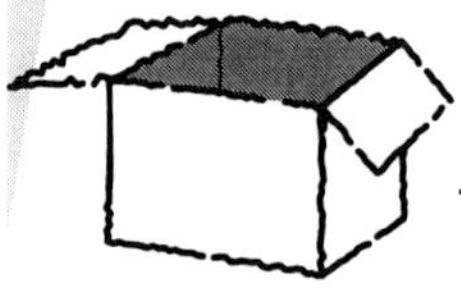 ___ ___ ___

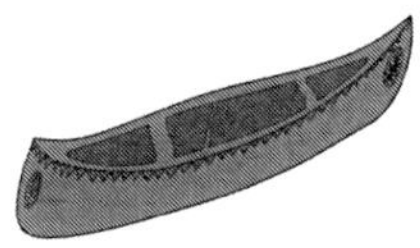 ___ ___ ___ ___ ___

 ___ ___ ___ ___ ___ ___ ___

 ___ ___ ___ ___ ___

 ___ ___ ___ ___ ___ ___ ___ ___ ___ ___

 ___ ___ ___ ___ ___ ___

 ___ ___ ___ ___ ___ ___ ___

 ___ ___ ___ ___ ___ ___ ___

American Indians Today

Beginning with the first letter of each group of letters, cross out every other letter to discover some new words. You may not have heard of these before, but you can read all about them!

1. Many Indians live on these, but many more do not!

TRYELSDEBRNVJAOTPIPOWNASX

____

2. Many Indians have been poor for a long time because for many years the government took away their lands and their ability to make a living.

TPKOOVWEBRNTXYA

____

3. Many Indians have been studying hard at school and going to college in order to earn more money. Education helps the Indians make their lives better. These Native Americans are working to become:

TSJUMCBCFEYSMSOFPUVL

____

4. This is a big term that means Native Americans have worked hard to get the U.S. government to let them rule themselves. This means that they have their own laws and make their own decisions. They are like a separate country inside the U.S.! Now, try and see if you can get your parents to give you the same thing!

TSGENLBF **JDGEETSEWRAMCIHNUAKTYIKOTNU**

_________________ _______________________________________

Fast Fact

What do Indians work as today?

- doctors
- nurses
- factory workers
- artists
- lawyers
- actors

The same kinds of jobs any American might work at!

Native Americans Move to the City!

Solve the code to discover the mystery words!

A	B	C	D	E	F	G	H	I	J	K	L	M
✷	❀	⌘	♣	➽	♥	❢	✯	✂	✆	☛	✈	✉
N	**O**	**P**	**Q**	**R**	**S**	**T**	**U**	**V**	**W**	**X**	**Y**	**Z**
✿	☆	◆	✡	✏	❥	☎	✒	✙	✖	✍	✠	✓

1. During the 1950s and 1960s, the American government paid Indians to leave their homes on reservations and move to cities to get jobs. If cities are sometimes called urban areas, then these brave Indians were called:

___ ___ ___ ___ ___   ___ ___ ___ ___ ___ ___ ___

✒ ✏ ❀ ✷ ✿   ✂ ✿ ♣ ✂ ✷ ✿ ❥

2. Many Indians chose to stay on their reservations and not move to the city. They thought that if they moved to the city, they would lose the way of life that their parents and ancestors had taught. These Indians called themselves:

___ ___ ___ ___ ___ ___ ___ ___ ___ ___ ___   ___ ___ ___ ___ ___ ___ ___

✏ ➽ ❥ ➽ ✏ ✙ ✷ ☎ ✂ ☆ ✿   ✂ ✿ ♣ ✂ ✷ ✿ ❥

3. Native Americans who moved to cities lived close to each other. They tried to keep their way of life as much as possible. They did not want to forget their religion, native art, or music. They did not want to lose their:

___ ___ ___ ___ ___ ___ ___

⌘ ✒ ✈ ☎ ✒ ✏ ➽

4. Are you afraid of heights? Many people are. The Mohawk Indians are not! Many of them work hundreds of feet above the city to build steel frames for skyscrapers. People who do this work above the city are:

___ ___ ___ ___ ___   ___ ___ ___ ___ ___ ___ ___

❥ ☎ ➽ ➽ ✈   ✖ ☆ ✏ ☛ ➽ ✏ ❥

5. Today urban Indians and reservation Indians come together to celebrate their culture. They share ideas and stories. They dance and beat drums. They make and sell Indian jewelry. During these celebrations, Indians remember how much they have to be proud of! These big parties are called

___ ___ ___ ___ ___ ___ ___

◆ ☆ ✖ ✖ ☆ ✖ ❥